Kes Gray

DAISY

and the trouble with

GIANTS

RED FOX

RED FOX

UK | USA | Canada | Ireland | Australia
India | New Zealand | South Africa

Red Fox is part of the Penguin Random House group of companies
whose addresses can be found at global.penguinrandomhouse.com.

www.penguin.co.uk
www.puffin.co.uk
www.ladybird.co.uk

Penguin
Random House
UK

First published 2008
This edition published 2020

001

Set in VAG Rounded Light 15pt/23pt
Printed in Great Britain by Clays Ltd, Elcograf S.p.A.

A CIP catalogue record for this book is available from the British Library

ISBN: 978–1–782–95975–5

All correspondence to
Red Fox, Penguin Random House Children's
One Embassy Gardens, 8 Viaduct Gardens
London SW11 7BW

For Geraldine, a GIANT
amongst writers!

Chapter 1

The **trouble with giants** is they shouldn't live at the top of magic beanstalks.

If giants didn't live at the top of magic beanstalks, then what happened today wouldn't have happened in the first place.

Or the second place.

Or any of the places in Nanny and Grampy's garden.

Nanny wouldn't have got cross.

Mum wouldn't have got cross.

Grampy wouldn't have got cross.

No one would have got cross.

You can't blame me if magic beans don't sparkle. Magic beans would be really easy to spot if they did sparkle like magic. But they don't.

Which ISN'T MY FAULT!!!

Chapter 2

I'd LOVE to meet a real giant.

Giants have giant shoes with giant buckles, giant clothes with giant buttons, giant front doors with giant doorbells, and inside their castles they have giant tables with plates full of giant food.

If I was a giant, I'd eat crunchy creams as big as tractor tyres! And I'd keep them in a biscuit tin as big as a house!

If I wanted a drink, I wouldn't pour my orange squash into a glass,

I'd pour it into a swimming pool! And then I'd drink it with a huge giant straw! I reckon a giant's straw would be as long as a ladder at least! Even longer probably! Maybe even as long as two drainpipes!

I bet a giant could empty a swimming pool of orange squash in about two sucks!! *One* suck if it was lemonade! Because lemonade is the best drink in the world.

Meeting a giant for real would be soooooo good! He could pick me up and put me on his shoulder and we could go everywhere together.

We'd have giant adventures and everything. When we got thirsty we could drink giant lemonades, and when we got hungry we could eat giant crunchy creams.

Or custard creams. I don't really mind.

That's another **trouble with giants**. They get REALLY hungry and REALLY thirsty.

Which is why they go *Fee Fi Fo Fum.*

The **trouble with saying *Fee Fi Fo Fum*** is only giants should be allowed to say it.

Otherwise it can end up getting quite rude.

In storytime at school on Friday, Jack Beechwhistle said "Fee Fi Fo Fum" really loudly. And then he said, "Daniel Baines is a stinky bum."

Which rhymes. But it isn't very nice.

Mrs Peters, our teacher, doesn't like it if you shout out in class.

Especially if you shout *"Fee Fi Fo Fum, Daniel Baines is a stinky bum."*

She said if Jack Beechwhistle didn't say sorry to Daniel Baines straight away, then there wouldn't be any more storytimes on a Friday ever again. For any of us!

Which is really unfair, because why should me and all my friends not get any more stories just because of what Jack Beechwhistle said?

That's the **trouble with Jack Beechwhistle.** He can't control his words. Especially during storytimes.

The **trouble with storytimes at school** is we only get one story.

I wish we got a hundred stories! And I wish all the stories were about giants!!

Mrs Peters is really good at reading stories. She does different voices and everything. When my mum reads me stories at bedtime she does the same voices for everything, so like if there's a princess and a prince in the story they have the same-sounding voice, even when one's a man and one's a woman.

Which isn't right really.

Mrs Peters does princess voices, prince voices, king voices, witch voices, wolf voices and even frog voices.

My mum just does mum voices. But I do still like her reading stories to me.

On Friday Mrs Peters read us the story of *Jack and the Beanstalk*. It was really good, except for when Jack Beechwhistle started Fee-Fi-Fo-Fumming all over the place.

The story of *Jack and the Beanstalk* has got all sorts of really exciting things in it, like the giant (he's the best bit) and a hen that lays golden eggs, and a harp that sings all by itself, and golden treasure,

and a magic beanstalk, plus a really sharp axe!

Mrs Peters did all the voices and everything.

Apart from the beanstalk and the sharp axe.

The **trouble with beanstalks and sharp axes** is they can't speak.

Which means they didn't say anything during the story.

But everyone else did.

Including Jack Beechwhistle.

Mrs Peters put the book down when Jack Beechwhistle started Fee-Fi-Fo-Fumming.

She said just because the hero in the story happened to be called Jack too, there was no excuse for silliness.

Or shouting.

Jack Beechwhistle is always being silly. And shouty.

And rude.

Anyway, he did say sorry to Daniel in the end. So we will still get stories at school next Friday afternoon.

I hope Jack Beechwhistle doesn't. I hope he has to stand outside the classroom and be really sorry.

Because I don't think he was sorry at all to Daniel Baines.

Neither does my best friend Gabby.

Chapter 3

On the way home from school after our *Jack and the Beanstalk* story, Gabby and me pretended we were giants too!

Gabby changed her name to Gabby the Great and I changed my name to Daisy the Enormous. (I couldn't think of a gianty word that begins with D. Neither could my mum.)

Apart from Dinosaur.

But Daisy the Dinosaur didn't sound right. Plus dinosaurs aren't like giants.

Well, they *are* giant, but they don't look like giants.

So I went for Enormous.

Pretending to be giants is brilliant fun! Gabby and me did great big giant footsteps instead of normal ones!

All the way home!

We pretended the cracks in the pavement were roads! We pretended that all the ants by our feet were cars and all the gnats in the air were helicopters.

That's what happens when you are a giant. Everything around you goes really teensy, because you're so tall and high up.

Someone had thrown an orange-squash carton on the pavement so we pretended it was a really tall building.

And then we trod on it!

Then Gabby saw some chewed-up chewing gum on the pavement and pretended it was a really big mountain!

Then she trod on that too!

The **trouble with pretending chewed-up chewing gum is a mountain** is if you tread on it, it gets stuck to your shoe. REALLY STUCK.

Especially when it's a hot day.

Mum said that on hot days things warm up in the sunshine, and when they warm up they go all soft and sticky. Especially things like chewing gum. You should never tread on chewing gum on a hot day. Especially chewed-up chewing gum.

Actually, Mum said it's probably better not to tread on chewing gum at all. Even on cold days.

Gabby said she had no choice, because she had changed her name again. This time she was called Gabby the Mountain Crusher, and so when she saw the mountain she just had to tread on it.

Mum said she would have to be Gabby the Foot Scraper now, because the only way to get the chewing gum off would be to scrape the bottom of her shoe along the pavement all the way home.

She did look funny!

When we got to Gabby's house, Gabby and I promised we would play giants all weekend! I said I would go to Gabby's house to play on Saturday, and Gabby said she would come to my house to play on Sunday.

That's when my mum told me we

could only play giants together on Saturday. Because on Sunday me and my mum were going to my nanny and grampy's for lunch.

In our new second-hand car.

Me and my mum quite often go to my nanny and grampy's for Sunday lunch. Mum says it gives her a break.

I'm not sure what from though.

The **trouble with going to my nanny and grampy's for Sunday lunch** is sometimes I wish Gabby could come with us.

I really wished Gabby could come with us this Sunday, because playing giants properly takes two days at least.

But Mum said Gabby wouldn't be able to come with us this Sunday. She wanted to get used to driving our new second-hand car before she started giving people lifts in it.

That's the **trouble with new second-hand cars**. Green ones aren't as easy to drive as red ones.

I said that if Gabby and me put our seat belts on and closed our eyes all the way there, we would be fine.

But Mum said that wouldn't be necessary. And anyway we would have to give Nanny more notice.

My nanny makes the best gravy in the world, plus she gives me loads of roast potatoes.

Trouble is though, if you don't tell her at least six weeks before that someone else is coming to lunch, she'll get into a bit of a tizz.

Gabby says her nanny gets her roast potatoes out of a bag in the freezer. And her Yorkshire puddings.

But my nanny makes her Yorkshire puddings and potatoes herself!

I love going to my nanny and grampy's house any day of the week. They've got a shed with real mice holes in, plus they've got apple trees and plum trees, and a wheelbarrow!

The **trouble with wheelbarrows** is sometimes they squeak.

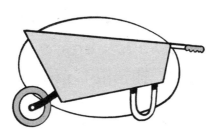

My grampy's wheelbarrow really squeaks. He says it isn't the wheelbarrow, it's the mice in the shed trying to trick us. But it isn't. It's my grampy trying to trick me!

Sometimes my grampy puts me in the wheelbarrow and takes me to London. Not real London. Pretend London. We pretend that he's my taxi driver and then off we go. London is the patio, and Buckingham Palace is the swing seat next to the red flowers.

Going to Nanny and Grampy's is one of the best things in the world.

Except for when I do something really really wrong and get really really told off.

Like today.

Mum said we'll be lucky if we ever get invited back to Nanny and Grampy's after what I did today.

Even if I did say sorry. And even if it was a GIANT SORRY.

Chapter 4

The **trouble with playing giants with Gabby** is she always wants to be the giantest.

When I got to her house yesterday morning, I told her that I had changed my name to Daisy the Ginormous and that I was definitely the giantest giant because I had grown a hundred metres higher in the night.

Trouble was, that made her really jealous. So every time I said how tall I was, she said she was the same *and a bit*.

The **trouble with me saying I was a hundred skyscrapers high** was Gabby said she was a hundred skyscrapers high *and a bit*.

The **trouble with me saying I was two million trees high** was Gabby said she was two million trees high *and a bit*.

And the **trouble with me saying I was a zillion big red buses high** *and a bit* was Gabby then said she was a zillion big red buses high *and two bits*!!

Which made me really cross!

So I changed my name to Daisy the Giantest And No Returns!

Hah! Gabby *had* to be the smallest giant after that!

Mind you, *even then* she still said she would only be the smallest giant by *half a bit.*

Sigh.

Gabby's always doing things like that.

When her mum and dad heard us arguing in the lounge, they came in and said that we'd have to play something else if we couldn't stop arguing.

But there was NO WAY we were going to ever play anything else. Playing giants is far too much fun!

So we stopped arguing.

And we went upstairs to play giants in Gabby's bedroom.

Gabby's bedroom is perfect for playing giants in. We pretended her bed was our castle, her wardrobe was the castle kitchen and her pillows were white fluffy clouds.

You need white fluffy clouds on the floor to pretend your castle is really high up.

Then we did a giant magic spell on all Gabby's toys and turned them into really good gianty things.

We had much better things than a hen that lays golden eggs. We had a teddy that gave us golden money, a monkey that laid golden bananas, a dolly that cried golden tears, and a golden dice that made everything six times more golden if you threw a six!

Except the **trouble with sixes** is they are a bit hard to get.

So we changed it to ten times more golden whatever number we threw.

In about five minutes we were rich!

The **trouble with being rich** is Gabby always wants to be richest.

Gabby said she was definitely the richest giant because the magic monkey had laid a bigger bunch of golden bananas for her than for me.

But I told her that the magic dolly who cried golden tears had done a ginormous 'normous teardrop for me, PLUS the teddy had given me a whole bank full of golden money.

Which made me the richest.

Then we started arguing again.

The **trouble with arguing again** is it made Gabby's dad come into the bedroom.

When he looked round the door at us, he did a giant huff and puff and said, "WHAT NOW?!"

I don't think he was pretending to be a giant, his huff and puff just came out that size.

Before I could say anything, Gabby said I wasn't being fair.

She'd let me be the biggest giant and NOW I wanted to be the RICHEST giant AS WELL!

Which wasn't true! It's not my fault if the magic dolly did bigger golden tears for me. Or if the magic teddy had been to the bank. But Gabby's dad folded his arms and did another giant huff and puff.

Then he went on Gabby's side and asked me if I wouldn't mind letting Gabby be the richest giant, seeing as I was the tallest giant.

So I HAD to say yes. She could be the richest giant. But only by half a golden banana.

Chapter 5

Once we'd sorted out who was the richest giant and who was the tallest giant, we got on really well.

Gabby changed her name to Mary the Massive and I changed mine to Tina the Terrifically Tall.

Gabby's dad said he'd never heard of a lady giant before, and he was sure a lady giant would be much scarier than a man giant.

But he was wrong.

Lady giants aren't scary at all.

Lady giants are really beautiful. And really kind.

The **trouble with man giants** is they look really ugly and fierce.

So everyone gets scared of them.

In Mrs Peters' stories, normal-sized people run away from man giants all the time. That's because the man giant always has hairs coming out of his nose and his ears, plus he has bobbly bits all over his face too.

And wonky teeth.

If man giants wore make-up or had proper washes with proper soap, or went to the dentist and brushed their hair a bit more, they'd probably look much nicer. Then everyone wouldn't run away.

Gabby says it's because giants are so big that people run away from them. But she's wrong. Because people don't run away from trees, do they? And they're one of the biggest things you can get.

Someone else who is big and fierce in Mrs Peters' stories is the troll.

The **trouble with trolls** is they don't live anywhere nearly as nice as a castle in the sky. Trolls live under smelly old bridges.

The **trouble with living under smelly old bridges** is it makes you smell smelly and old too.

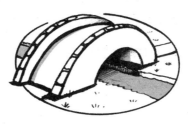

It makes you smell of seaweed and fish, plus if the river floods, you're going to get really wet socks.

The **trouble with wet socks** is they really smell. Especially smelly old trolls' wet socks.

If I'd been a Billy Goat Gruff, I'd have waited till the river flooded to cross the bridge safely. I'd have sneaked up to the bridge and quickly poured loads of shampoo and bubble bath into the river. That way the shampoo and bubbles would have cleaned the troll who was hiding underneath, plus when the water got really high, the soap suds would have gone right into his eyes so he couldn't see.

If a troll can't see you, it's easy peasy lemon squeezy to cross his bridge without being eaten.

Trouble is, I'm not sure if billy goats use shampoo.

Princesses who live in towers do. Mrs Peters told us about one in a fairy story. Her name was Rapunzel, which is a really bad name for a princess. And really long too.

But not as long as her hair.

Rapunzel's hair was the longest in the world. Which means she must have been an expert on shampoos.

Whenever she let her hair down to let princes climb up to see her, it was always REALLY nice and golden and shiny. It never had any tangles ever.

The **trouble with tangles** is they really hurt.

Especially if your mum yanks too hard with the hairbrush.

I'm not sure if the princess in the tower had a mum. If she did, she didn't live there. The princess had to do all her own washing and brushing and hair-drying.

So she must have known a lot about shampoos.

And conditioners.

My mum always makes me have shampoo AND conditioner.

I still sometimes get tangles though.

In our bathroom in our castle in the sky, Gabby and me had a cupboard full of giant bathroom things. Including bubble bath that made bubbles the size of the world!

We had giant singing soap, giant musical toothbrushes and giant cotton buds that did a dance when you clicked your fingers.

Except the **trouble with clicking your fingers** is Gabby can't do it.

So we clapped our hands instead.

I was the loudest clapper and Gabby was second loudest.

Except she said her claps were the giantest.

But we decided not to argue about it.

I definitely had the biggest lipstick though. My giant lipstick was a hundred metres long!

The **trouble with giant lipsticks** is once you've done your lips there is still loads left over.

So after we'd made ourselves look really beautiful, we used them to decorate the castle. Gabby coloured the castle walls orange with her lipstick, and I coloured the castle roof red with mine. But even once we'd coloured all the doors and floors too, we still had some giant lipstick left over! So we coloured the dungeon in as well.

Once our lipsticks had run out we were really hungry again.

So we ate some chocolate skyscrapers!

Chocolate skyscrapers are a giant's favourite sweet. They look like chocolate flakes, but they're as big as the actual skyscrapers you see on telly!

Gabby said she wished a real giant would eat a chocolate skyscraper right above her house. Then when he bit into it, giant crumbs would crumble off, fall through the clouds and land right in her back garden.

Then we'd have all the chocolate we could ever want. For life!

I said I'd rather the giant bought a giant strawberry dib-dab and then sneezed on it.

Then all the sherbet would fly out of the giant packet, fall through the clouds and cover our gardens like snow!

We could play snowballs with sherbet!

If it would roll into a ball.

Gabby said a giant's sherbet wouldn't roll into a ball. Unless his sneeze had made it really sticky.

That's the **trouble with giant's sherbet.** You go off it after that.

Chapter 6

After we'd eaten our chocolate skyscrapers we were still hungry, so we decided we'd cook a giant omelette.

The **trouble with giant omelettes** is you need three zillion eggs to cook one.

For our recipe, we needed a hundred lorries of milk and ten shops

of butter too. But luckily we'd been shopping so we had everything we needed in our giant fridge.

You should have seen the size of the bowl we used to mix everything up in! It was bigger than a football stadium! And you should have seen the size of the spoons we used for whisking!

Gabby's wooden spoon was eighty tree trunks long and mine was eighty-one! (But I didn't tell her.)

The **trouble with making a giant omelette** is all that giant whisking makes you really thirsty.

So, after every three whisks, I drank a swimming pool of lemonade.

And Gabby drank a swimming pool of cherry Coke!

It was Gabby who did a giant burp first though, not me.

I said she shouldn't do giant burps because her mum and dad might hear us and come and tell us off.

But they didn't hear us. So I did some giant burps too!

Gabby did thunder burps, which are really loud. I did volcano burps, which are even louder.

But the **trouble with volcano burps** is mine started an earthquake above the clouds!

Everything in our magic castle started to shake!

Including me and Gabby!

I shook all the way out of the castle kitchen, past the giant omelette bowl, out of the front door and nearly into the dungeon! Gabby shook all the way past the giant fridge, bumped into the omelette bowl, tipped it over and accidentally covered herself in giant omelette mixture. Which meant she looked like a giant omelette herself!

"FEE FI FO FUM!" she said in a Mary the Massive voice. "I'M A MASSIVE OMELETTE, YUM, YUM, YUM!!!!!"

Then she started walking round the magic castle doing giant omelette noises.

So then I tried to eat her.

The **trouble with trying to eat a giant omelette with legs** is they never let you catch them.

I chased Gabby out of the castle, down the hallway, through her mum and dad's bedroom, down the stairs and right the way into the lounge.

I chased her twice round the settee and three times round the armchairs, but still couldn't catch her.

Until she tripped over the wastepaper bin and nearly hit her head on the telly.

That's when her mum told us it was time for lunch.

Chapter 7

The **trouble with magic baked beans on toast** is there's no such thing.

Gabby's mum and dad said there might be, but they don't really under-stand about giants. Or magic beans.

A magic bean would never work if it was covered in tomato sauce.

When I was having baked beans on toast at Gabby's, her dad said the magic bean in *Jack and the Beanstalk* might have been a baked bean, but I know it definitely wasn't.

The magic bean in *Jack and the Beanstalk* was bigger and shinier. Mrs Peters showed us a picture of it in class.

I really wish there was such a thing as magic baked beans, then I wouldn't have got into trouble at Nanny and Grampy's today.

Mum could have just gone to the supermarket this morning and bought me a whole tin full of magic baked beans.

Then I could have washed the tomato sauce off and grown as many magic beanstalks as I wanted.

Gabby told her dad to stop being silly about magic baked beans or we would both put a giant spell on him.

Gabby's mum asked if we could turn him into a handsome prince, but we said no, we would turn him into something much more horrible.

Gabby wanted to turn him into a giant slug, but I said we should turn him into a giant pea. Then roll him down a mountain. Or off a cliff!

Gabby's dad left the table after that.

The **trouble with Gabby's mum** is she doesn't know anything about giants either.

When we asked her if she'd ever heard of a lady giant, she said she hadn't, but she was sure they must be out there somewhere. She said there must be lady giants, otherwise all the man giants wouldn't have any clothes to wear.

The **trouble with giants' clothes** is they are absolutely huge!

Their socks are about twenty metres long, their vests are about the size of a hundred bedcovers, and their shirts are big enough to cover a whole town!

Gabby's mum said it would probably take her two weeks to iron one pair of giant's trousers. Three weeks if he wanted a crease in both legs.

I said I didn't think lady giants did ironing. If giants have got magic harps that sing to them and hens that lay golden eggs for them, then they're bound to have magic ironing boards that do all their ironing for them too.

Gabby's mum said if we ever got to meet a lady giant, could we ask her if she could borrow her magic ironing board once a week?

And if she had a magic tea towel, could she borrow that too?

We said we'd ask, but **the trouble with lady giants** is they're even harder to meet than man giants.

Especially if you haven't got a magic bean!

Chapter 8

The **trouble with not having a magic bean** is it's impossible to grow a magic beanstalk if you haven't got one.

If you haven't got a magic beanstalk, then you'll never get all the way up into the clouds.

If you can't get all the way up to the clouds, then you'll never get to see a real giant's castle.

When Gabby and me went into the garden after our baked beans on toast, we could see the clouds high up in the sky above us, but we couldn't get anywhere near high enough to see through them.

I got my eyes up to the top of Gabby's fence, but Gabby's legs started to wobble, so she had to put me down.

Gabby said there was only one thing for it. We would have to find a magic bean of our own.

So we stopped playing giants for a while and went on a magic bean hunt.

The **trouble with looking for magic beans** is you should really have a cow with you.

If you have a cow with you like in *Jack and the Beanstalk,* then old ladies will just come straight up to you and say, "Hey, that's a nice cow you've got there. Would you like to swap it for some magic beans?"

First of all we checked the flowerbeds for cows. But there weren't any.

Then we looked in the bushes for old ladies. But there weren't any of those either.

The only thing that was old in Gabby's garden was some mouldy birdseed hanging from a wire thing in her tree.

Gabby said that in winter her mum puts nice new birdseed in the wire thing so the birds can get something to eat when it's snowing.

Trouble is, the birds can't get their beaks right down to the bottom of the wire thing, so some of the birdseed goes mouldy.

That's the **trouble with birds' beaks.** They aren't long enough in winter.

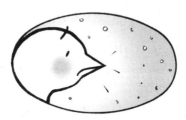

Once we hadn't found any cows or old ladies, we looked for farmers. Because farmers sometimes have cows and an old farmer might know an old lady.

But the **trouble with looking for young or old farmers in Gabby's back garden** is it needs to be a farm really.

Farms have loads of farmers and loads of cows. Gabby's garden doesn't. Gabby's garden doesn't even have even a small cat like Tiptoes.

There is grass in Gabby's back garden and I'm sure cows would really like it if they knew where it was, but Gabby's garden doesn't have a back gate either. So even if the cows knew where Gabby's grass was, they'd never be able to get in.

Neither would old ladies with magic beans.

Unless they came in through the front door of Gabby's house, like I did.

But I don't think Gabby's mum and dad would like that. Especially the cows.

Gabby said there might be some magic beans in her dad's shed.

But there was only a dartboard and a lawnmower. And neither of them were magic.

There were no magic beans under the *sun lounger,* no magic beans in the *watering can,* no magic beans in the *flower pots,* none in the *flowerbeds,* none on the *patio,* none on the *window ledges,* none near the *fish pond* and none anywhere else in Gabby's garden.

It was sooooooo frustrating!

We reeeeeaaaaaallllllllllly wanted to find a magic bean. But we couldn't find one anywhere!

So we went back to pretending to be giants instead.

CHAPTER 9

The **trouble with playing giants outside in the garden** is you're not allowed to use Gabby's pillows.

Gabby's mum said Gabby's pillows belonged on her bed and we weren't allowed to put them on the lawn because we would make them dirty.

So we had to put them back.

The **trouble with putting pillows back** is it means you don't have any white fluffy clouds.

Gabby's mum said we could use sun-lounger cushions as clouds if we wanted to, but Gabby's sun-lounger cushions are green with swirly flowers on. So they didn't look very good.

Then Gabby had a brilliant idea.

Instead of pretending we were giants living in a castle high up in the sky, we could pretend we had come down the beanstalk and were giants living on the ground!

So we did!

I came down the beanstalk first because I was the best climber-downer (but I didn't tell Gabby), and then Gabby came down next.

Then we took it in turns to think of giant things to do!

First of all we went shopping.

If you're going shopping and you've got giant legs, you can step over anything. Gabby stepped straight over her garden fence and marched all the way down the road to the shopping precinct.

Because my legs were slightly longer it meant I could step right over Gabby's HOUSE!

So I did! Then I marched all the way down the road to the shopping precinct!

It was brilliant!! Plus I got there just before Gabby did too.

The shopping precinct is where our mums go to do the shopping. But we didn't take our mums, because they're too teensy.

The **trouble with being a teensy mum** is you might get trodden on just like that.

I wouldn't want to squash my mum! Even if she did tell me off at Nanny and Grampy's today.

So we went to the shops on our own.

The first place we went shopping in the shopping precinct was the toyshop! You should have seen all the teensy people's faces when we bent down and pulled the roof of the toyshop right off!

They weren't scared because we had nice lipstick on, but they were really surprised! Everyone pointed up at us, and said, "WOW, LOOK AT THOSE BEAUTIFUL GIANTS! THEY'RE ENORMOUS!"

Then the toyshop owner came out and said, "Can I help you, beautiful giants?"

"YES!" said Wendy the Whopping (which was Gabby's new pretend giant's name). "YES, you CAN help us, Mr Toyshop Owner! We would like to buy all of your toys!"

"ALL OF THEM?" said the toyshop owner.

"YES," said Wendy, "ALL of them. And here's enough golden bananas to pay for them."

Then we scooped all of the toys in the shop into a giant carrier bag, and went down the road to somewhere else.

"FEE FI FO FUM!" I said in a really loud giant's voice. "I WANT TO BUY SOME BUBBLE GUM!"

You should have seen everyone's faces when we lifted the roof off the sweetshop! All the teensy children inside hid behind the sweetshop counter when they saw us, but then they realized we were friendly so they came out.

"How much bubble gum do you want?" asked the sweetshop owner.

"ALL OF IT!" I said.

"All of it?" he said.

"YES, ALL OF IT!" I said.

"AND ALL OF YOUR CHOCOLATE!" said Wendy the Whopping.

"AND ALL OF YOUR DIB-DABS!" said Hannah the Highest (which was me, because I'd changed my name as well).

"IN FACT, MR SWEETSHOP OWNER," I said, "GIVE US *ALL OF YOUR SWEETS!*"

All the teensy-weensy children in the sweetshop groaned, and the sweetshop owner fell down on his knees.

"But how will you pay me?" he cried.

"IN GOLDEN BANANAS!" I shouted. "IN GOLDEN BANANAS AND WHOPPING GOLDEN DOLLY'S TEARS!"

"But we won't have any sweets if you eat them all!" said all the teensy children. "Please leave some sweets for us!"

When we looked down, we realized that some of

the teensy children were our friends from school. So, because we were really kind giants as well as beautiful ones, we gave a free bag of sweets to all the children in the shop.

Apart from Jack Beechwhistle.

I picked Jack Beechwhistle up by his ear and threw him a hundred miles into the air, right through the clouds, right into our castle and right into our dungeon.

"WHERE SHALL WE GO NEXT, HANNAH THE HIGHISH?" said Wendy the Whopping.

"HIGH*EST*, NOT HIGH*ISH*," I roared. "NEXT WE WILL GO TO THE SWIMMING POOL!"

CHAPTER 10

The **trouble with swimming pools**
is the doors are nowhere near big
enough for a giant to get in. So we
had to pull the roof off that too.

You should have seen everyone's
faces when we looked down on all
the teensy swimmers! They all went,
"WOW!!!!!"

And then they started to shiver.

Not because they were frightened, but because they were getting cold.

That's the **trouble with giants pulling the roof off swimming pools.** All the people inside get goosebumps.

"Put the roof back on, please!" shivered all the teensy swimmers. "It's freezing in here!"

"I'M AFRAID WE CAN'T!" I shouted back. "IF WE DON'T TAKE THE ROOF

OFF THE SWIMMING POOL, WE CAN'T COME IN FOR A PADDLE!"

Then everyone screamed and got out of the swimming pool fast.

First Wendy the Whopping took her tights off and then Hannah the Highest took her socks off. Then we hung them over the top diving board to stop them from getting wet.

Then we got in!

And guess what?!

The deep end only came up to our ankles!!!

Once all the teensy swimmers realized that we were really kind giants, they got back into the pool.

Liberty Pearce did handstands off my fingernail into the water, and Dylan did hundred-metre dive-bombs off Wendy the Whopping's shoulders. It was brilliant!

When we left the swimming pool, all the children really thanked us, plus then we put the roof back on so they didn't get goosebumps any more.

Wendy the Whopping said it was a good job she hadn't got thirsty or she might have had to drink the swimming-pool water instead of paddling in it.

I said that wasn't a very good idea.

The **trouble with drinking swimming-pool water** is someone might have weed in it.

My mum says some children wee in swimming pools without anyone knowing. She said some swimming pools can get invisible wee germs in them, and that you have to be really careful not to let the water go in your mouth when you're swimming.

Wendy the Whopping said giants are far too giant to be got by a teensy-weensy-weensy-weensy wee germ.

But my mum says germs don't care if you're big or small. If you let them get inside you, they will get you big time. That's why you must always keep your mouth shut when you're swimming.

After our giant paddle, me and Wendy the Whopping went for a rest.

The **trouble with giants resting** is you should have seen everyone's faces when we lay down in the park!

Wendy the Whopping's body stretched from the boating lake right across to the swings on the other side of the park!

My body stretched from the boating lake right across to the slide. (Which is just a bit further than the swings.)

The **trouble with giants being sooooo big** is when you lie down in the park, it means the park keeper can't mow the grass properly.

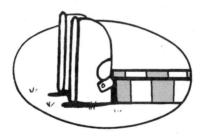

Which means he either has to go over you, or round you.

The park keeper in our park went over us, which really tickled our tummies.

The **trouble with ticklish giants** is if they laugh too loud, ANYTHING can happen.

Buildings can fall down, the church steeple can fall off, all the leaves can fall off the trees, and all the squirrels will fall off their branches.

That's exactly what happened in our park. Plus the park keeper's false teeth fell out!

So we had to get up and go somewhere else, because he was really cross.

Wendy the Whopping said the cinema would be a good place to go, but I said when we pulled the roof off, all the light would get in and we wouldn't be able to see the film.

That's the **trouble with films at the cinema.** You have to watch them in the dark.

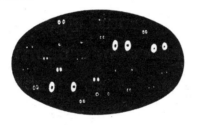

So I said, "Let's go somewhere we've never been before. Let's go somewhere really different! FOLLOW ME!" I said. "To the car crushers!"

Chapter 11

My mum says that when cars get really old and won't work any more, they go to a place to be crushed! That's where our red car went before we got our new second-hand green one.

To the car crushers!

My mum says at the car crushers there's a big tall crane that picks up the broken cars and drops them into a great big crusher thingy that crushes and squeezes the broken car until it doesn't look like a car any more.

It looks like a great big metal

sugar lump!

It takes lots of super-strong power to crush a car into a sugar lump.

Unless you're a giant!

You should have seen everyone's faces when we turned up at the car crushers!

"GIANTS DON'T NEED CRANES TO PICK UP CARS!" I said. "WE'RE HANNAH THE HIGHEST AND WENDY THE WHOPPING AND WE CAN PICK UP CARS JUST LIKE THIS!"

Everyone at the car crushers watched in amazement as I put down my shopping bags and picked up our old red car in both hands!

"GIANTS DON'T NEED A CAR-CRUSHING THINGY TO CRUSH CARS WITH EITHER," I said. "I CAN DO IT WITH MY FINGERS JUST LIKE THIS!"

Then all the teensy people who worked at the car crushers watched in amazement as I crushed our old red car into a sugar-lump shape with my bare hands!

As the car squashed inside my fingers, loads of rust fell off it and sprinkled like pepper onto all the people below.

But we didn't eat anyone. We just took it in turns to crush cars with our bare hands instead!

Crushing cars with your hands is BRILLIANT! Wendy the Whopping crushed two thousand and fifty cars in hers. And I crushed two thousand and fifty-one in mine.

Plus an army tank.

Everyone at the car crushers thought we were the best car crushers ever, because we squashed everything much smaller than they ever could have done.

Plus their car-crusher thingy couldn't do army tanks.

The **trouble with crushing army tanks with your bare hands** is it gives you giant splinters.

So we went to the doctor's next.

You should have seen everyone's faces when we pulled the roof off the doctor's surgery!

The doctor nearly fainted when he saw us!

"What seems to be the problem?" he said to us.

"WE'VE GOT GIANT CAR SPLINTERS!" said Wendy.

"AND I'VE GOT A REALLY GIANT TANK SPLINTER," I said.

"Then you'll have to go to the hospital," said the doctor. "The hospital's tweezers are much bigger than mine. I only do teensy people's splinters."

So we put the roof back on the doctor's and went to the hospital.

You should have seen everyone's faces when we walked down the high street!

You should have seen everyone's faces when we pulled the roof off the hospital!

One patient with a broken leg was so surprised to see us, he fell out of bed!

Trouble is, he didn't have a broken leg until he fell out of bed. He only had a sore throat.

All the teensy doctors and nurses in the hospital came running down the corridors to see us. They gave us giant X-rays, and then a hundred doctors lifted some giant tweezers and pulled our splinters out.

Then we felt better. So we went to the ice-cream parlour.

You should have seen the look on the lady's face when we pulled the roof off her shop!

"What flavour would you like?" she asked.

"ALL OF THEM!" I said.

"Except rum and raisin," said Wendy the Whopping. (Wendy the Whoppings don't like rum and raisin.) Hannah the Highests do. Hannah the Highests like every type of ice cream. All at once!

The **trouble with ice-cream parlours** is normal scoops are far too small for a giant.

"I think I'll need a bigger scoop," said the ice-cream-parlour lady.

"LEAVE IT TO ME!" I said, walking to America and pulling a great big satellite dish off one of their rocket-launching stations.

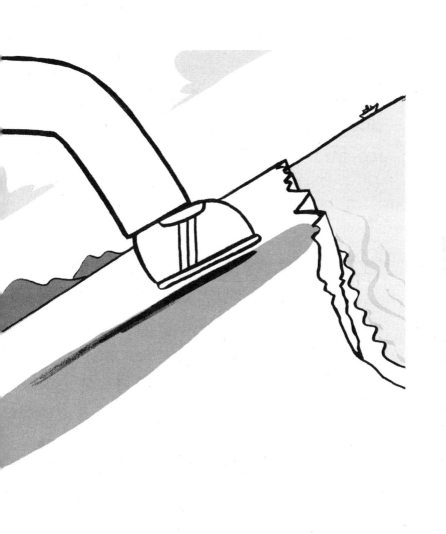

The **trouble with giant ice-cream bowls** is you need loads and loads of ice cream to fill them.

The ice-cream parlour lady only had about twelve normal-sized tubs in her freezer, which wasn't nearly enough ice cream at all.

"WE MUST WALK TO THE NORTH POLE!" said Wendy the Whopping. "There's a giant ice-cream factory there!"

So we did.

But we didn't take the ice-cream parlour lady with us. Because she was too teensy and she wouldn't have been able to keep up.

You should have seen Wendy the Whopping's face when I pulled the roof off the ice-cream factory!

Instead of teensy people, there were loads of teensy polar bears looking up. They all wore aprons and hats that said ICE-CREAM FACTORY on them.

Wendy the Whopping didn't know polar bears made ice cream.

I did.

When the polar bears saw that we were kind and beautiful giants, they offered to make us a special giant-sized ice cream each.

I had an orange lolly that was a hundred metres long and Wendy the Whopping had a cone with a chocolate flake in it as big as a tree!

The polar bears said that all their ice creams were free to giants and that we could have another one if we wanted. But we told them that we had to get back to England pretty soon.

I got back to England first and Wendy the Whopping got back to

England second. Then we had a race to see who could get back to Gabby's back garden first.

Gabby took ten seconds but I took five because I knew a short cut over some really tall buildings.

Gabby said I couldn't have taken five seconds, because walking from England to her back garden in five seconds was impossible.

Which means she was jealous again. But I didn't say anything because I didn't want to hurt her feelings.

Then she said I wasn't allowed to be the highest AND the strongest

AND the fastest giant as well.

So I said if she let me be the highest and the strongest and the fastest giant, next time we went to the North Pole she could have the nicest excitingest giantest ice cream.

But she said she had already had the nicest excitingest giantest ice cream, because cones with ice cream and flakes in are better than boring old lollies.

So I said lollies weren't boring.

But she said lollies WERE boring, especially orange lollies.

So I said mine wasn't normal orange, it was fizzy giant orange made to a special fizzy giant recipe.

So she said her flake had special giant sprinkles on it that changed flavour when you put them in your mouth.

Then I said my lolly had special giant sprinkles on too, but they were inside the lolly, so you couldn't see them.

Then she said I didn't.

So then I said I did.

And then she said I DIDN'T!

And then I said I DID!

AND THEN . . . Gabby's dad said my mum had just rung and that it was time for me to go home. So we had to stop arguing about ice creams after that.

And we had to stop pretending to be giants too. Which was probably a good thing.

Because Gabby was obviously getting tired.

CHAPTER 12

When I got home from Gabby's house, my mum asked if I'd had a good time.

I said apart from Gabby being a bit jealous, we'd had a brilliant time, and that pretending to be giants was the best thing on earth!

I said PLEEEEEEEAAAAAASSSSE could Gabby come with us to Nanny and Grampy's, because we still had loads more giant games we needed to play.

I soooooooooooooooo wish Mum

had said yes, because I'm sure I wouldn't have got into trouble at Nanny and Grampy's house if I'd had Gabby to play with.

Well, at least not THAT much trouble.

Trouble is, she didn't say yes.

She said no.

She said Gabby and I could play giants again at school on Monday instead.

I said Mrs Peters wouldn't let us.

But Mum said she didn't mean in the actual classroom during lessons. She meant we could play giants in the school playground at break time.

Which is nowhere near long enough to play giants.

That's the **trouble with break times at school.**

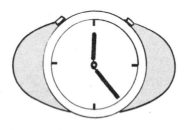

They're about five hours too short.

So I said, "DOUBLE PLEEEEEEEEASE, MUM, CAN GABBY COME WITH US TO NANNY AND GRAMPY'S?"

And then I said, "TRIPLE PLEEEEEEEEASE, MUM, CAN GABBY COME WITH US?!"

Then I tried a **"GIANT**

TRIPLEDIPPLEDOPPLE PLEEEEEEEASE, MUM, CAN GABBY COME WITH US?!!!!"

But Mum did one of her "no" faces.

There would be only two people going to Nanny and Grampy's for Sunday lunch this weekend.

One would be my mum.

One would be me.

And none would be Gabby.

Which WASN'T my fault!

CHAPTER 13

When I went to bed that night, Mum promised she would read me a story.

We didn't have *Jack and the Beanstalk* so she read me *Little Red Riding Hood* instead.

The **trouble with Little Red Riding Hood** is she was little.

If Little Red Riding Hood had been Big Red Riding Hood or, even better,

GIANT Red Riding Hood, the wolf would never have tried to eat her in the first place!

Even if the wolf had been REALLY, REALLY hungry, there's no way a normal-sized wolf could eat a giant Red Riding Hood.

He wouldn't even have enough room for her little toe.

That's the **trouble with wolves in fairy stories.** They are always trying to eat people.

Like the Three Little Pigs.

You see! *They* were little as well!

If the Three Little Pigs had been the Three GIANT Pigs, their houses would have been far too big for a wolf to blow down. Even the house made out of straw.

If Hansel and Gretel had been giant children, they could have eaten the candy house and the witch all in one go.

If you ask me, the **trouble with fairy stories** is there are too many little people in them, and not enough giants.

Especially giant pigs and giant children.

After Mum had finished reading me my bedtime story, I did the giantest yawn I'd ever done in my whole life. Not on purpose. It just came out.

Mum gave me a giant kiss goodnight and told me to have a dream about going to Sunday lunch at a GIANT nanny and grampy's.

She said to imagine how much bigger than the mountains the roast potatoes would be, and how high into the sky the Yorkshire puddings would rise!

So I did!

But by the time I got to the carrots I think I must have fallen asleep.

CHAPTER 14

When I woke up this morning, the first thing I thought of was giants! The second thing I thought of was the loo.

I was busting for a wee. (It must have been all those swimming pools of lemonade I drank when I was a giant yesterday!)

After I'd flushed the loo and washed my hands and gone downstairs, I saw my mum was already in the kitchen. Which is really unusual for a Sunday.

On Sundays, my mum usually lies in bed until at least ten o'clock. Because she's really lazy. But this morning she got up early to make a banoffee pie to take to Nanny's.

The **trouble with banoffee pies** is I really like the toffee and the cream and the biscuit but I'm not too keen on the bananas.

Bananas are *all right,* but I'd much rather Mum left the bananery bits out. Then it would be perfect.

Mum said that without the bananery bits it wouldn't be a banoffee pie at all. It would be an offee pie. And no one ever went to someone's for Sunday lunch with an offee pie. Especially a nanny and grampy's.

I said Nanny and Grampy wouldn't know we'd left the bananery bits out, because the bananery bits were hidden under the cream.

But Mum said they would know. Especially when they bit into it and tasted no banana.

That's the **trouble with banana.**

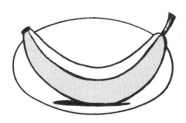

It tastes too much like banana.

So the bananery bits had to go in.

While Mum was making the toffee for the toffee bit of the pie, I had my breakfast.

The **trouble with breakfast** is no one does real boulders in a packet.

So I had to pretend my Rice Krispies were giant boulders instead. Every time I crunched, I imagined a giant mouthful of rocks crumbling between my teeth.

After I'd finished my boulders, I washed it all down with a lake full of cold milk and then went upstairs again to brush my giant teeth.

Then I started missing Gabby. If Gabby had been allowed to knock for me this morning, we could have played giants in my back garden at least until I left to go to Nanny and Grampy's. We might even have found a magic bean!

We could have grown our own beanstalk, changed our names again to something even more gianty, and gone on even more giant adventures, PLUS taken my pillows off my bed and taken them outside! (Well, maybe not outside, but somewhere quite near the back door.)

If Gabby had come round to my house this morning, we could have played all sorts of giant games.

But she didn't.

So we couldn't.

So I went back to being normal-sized again. And then I started getting really bored.

The **trouble with being normal-sized AND bored** is there's nothing anyone can do about it.

You just have to sit in a chair and be normal-sized and bored until it's time to go out.

You can get out of the chair if you want, but even if you do, you'll still be normal-sized and bored.

You can be normal-sized and bored looking out of a window, normal-sized and bored sitting on your bed, normal-sized and bored lying on the sofa . . . The only time this morning that I was normal-sized and not THAT bored was when I went into my back garden on my own without Gabby to look for magic beans again. But I couldn't find any.

So I went back to being bored again. (I was still normal-sized when I went out into the garden.)

By the time my mum had told me to get into our new second-hand car, my eyebrows had nearly dropped off I was so bored.

But when we arrived outside my nanny and grampy's house, I suddenly started to feel better!

CHAPTER 15

The **trouble with suddenly starting to feel better** is it makes your mum think that you weren't really bored in the first place.

That's the **trouble with going to Nanny and Grampy's**.

It makes people think you're a fibber.

When we got out of the car, I changed my face to half bored and half excited, but by the time I got to the front door it had gone all excited again.

I LOVE going to my nanny and grampy's for Sunday lunch!

I love the smell of gravy when we walk in, and the sound of their electric carving knife!

Except, when Grampy opened the door of his house today, there wasn't the smell of gravy or the sound of a knife.

There was the smell of burning and the sound of scraping!

Nanny had burned the Yorkshire puddings!

When we got inside, Grampy shut the front door and told us that they had bought a new cooker!

Not a new second-hand cooker. A new new cooker! They must be rich!

The **trouble with buying a new new cooker** is it takes a while to get used to all the new new knobs and new new switches.

Especially if you're as old old as my nanny.

When we went into the kitchen, Nanny was standing by the cooker waving smoke everywhere with an oven glove.

She had burned the Yorkshires, and the roast potatoes, and all the vegetables too, including the carrots, which is a real shame because carrots are really nice. Especially covered in Nanny's gravy.

Nanny said lunch had been slightly delayed and that she would have to do all the vegetables and all the Yorkshire puddings again.

Mum said not to worry, and that we would be quite happy to not have any Yorkshire puddings and vegetables at all.

But Nanny said, "Sunday lunch without Yorkshire puddings and vegetables?! Not in MY house!"

Then she said that lunch would be another hour at least, so we might as well all go outside into the garden to get away from the smoke.

And then she hit the oven with her oven glove.

Honest! Nanny told the oven right off!

The **trouble with hitting ovens with oven gloves** is ovens don't know you're telling them off.

Because ovens are metal.

Then Nanny called it a stupid oven. Which wouldn't work because ovens don't have ears either. So they can't hear you.

Mum said she would stay in the kitchen and help Nanny scrape the burned Yorkshire puddings out of the tray.

Grampy said he would go into the garden and pick some more runner beans.

YUP! I couldn't believe it either! That's exactly what he said!!!

"RUNNER BEANS!" I said.

"RUNNER BEANS! HAVE YOU GOT REAL RUNNER BEANS IN YOUR GARDEN, GRAMPY?"

And you'll never guess what Grampy said!

He said, "YES!"

CHAPTER 16

"Can I help? Can I help?" I said. "Can I help you pick some runner beans?!"

And guess what?

Grampy said I COULD!

He took a bowl out of the kitchen cupboard and said to me, "Come on then, Daisy. Fresh runner beans are delicious. You pick some from the bottom and I'll pick some from the top!"

Then I followed him out of the kitchen and into the garden!

The **trouble with my grampy's garden** is it can make you get quite excited. Especially as it's got beans in it.

It's much bigger than my garden and has a bird bath and a vegetable garden *and* even a GREENHOUSE!

My grampy's vegetables were over by the fence near the greenhouse.

Sometimes you could see where the actual vegetables were growing. Like if they were tomatoes, because tomatoes grow above the ground.

And sometimes you couldn't see where the actual vegetables were growing. Like potatoes and carrots. Because potatoes and carrots grow under the ground.

"Welcome to my vegetable garden, Daisy!" said Grampy, showing me where it was. "These are my tomatoes and these are my spring onions, these are my new potatoes, those are my carrots, these are my lettuces and these are my runner beans! Nanny and I grow all our own vegetables!" said Grampy.

"The tomatoes are green at the moment because they aren't ripe yet, but they'll be a lovely red colour in a month or so!"

Grampy was really pleased with his vegetables.

He said vegetables are fresher and tastier if you grow them in your own garden. Much fresher and tastier than if you buy them in a shop!

Then I asked Grampy if he would show me the runner beans. And guess what!

The runner beans weren't growing in nice straight rows at all!

They were growing up towards the sky on sticks!

Grampy called them "bamboo" sticks. He had pushed them into the ground just like an Indian tepee!

Grampy said runner beans grow up and up, and that the bamboo sticks gave them something to hold onto.

I told Grampy that I knew a lot about beans because I had listened to *Jack and the Beanstalk* at school.

I told him Gabby and me had spent the whole day yesterday playing giants and that we had spent ages and ages looking for a magic bean of our own. But we couldn't find any beans anywhere.

Apart from baked beans at lunch time. But they were covered in tomato sauce.

"Well, you'd better get picking, Daisy!" said Grampy. "We'll need at least twenty nice big runner beans for our Sunday lunch!"

So I did!

I picked my first ever actual runner bean! With my own fingers!

Grampy showed me how to do it first. He showed me how to lift up the leaves and look for the long green dangly things that were hidden underneath.

Then he pulled one off the stalk, slid his fingernail down the join at the side of the long green case, and pulled it open with the rest of his fingers.

You should have seen what was inside!

It wasn't just one runner bean. It was five! Five lovely, shiny, pink runner beans, with little black-and-brown dots and splodges on them.

Each bean was all snuggledy-puggledy inside its own smooth little dip, but if you pushed it with your thumb, it came out!

Grampy pushed a shiny pink bean out with his thumb and then gave it to me to hold!

"Is it magic?" I said.

"I doubt it!" he said.

So then I had a really good close-up look. It felt magic.

And it was definitely shiny, but it wasn't exactly sparkly.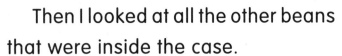

In fact it wasn't sparkly at all.

So it can't have been magic.

Then I looked at all the other beans that were inside the case.

None of them were magic either.

"Can we pick some more?" I asked.

"Pick away!" laughed Grampy. "We need nineteen more big ones for lunch."

So this time I got to pick my very own!

Grampy reached up to the very top of the bamboo sticks and I reached about up to the middle.

That's the **trouble with being about seven years old.** It doesn't make you about seven feet tall!

I couldn't wait to open up my own beans. The first one I opened had five shiny beans in! And the second one I opened had six!

But none of them were sparkly.

Which meant that none of them were magic either.

It was still really good though, because I'd never opened beans before.

Only then Grampy went and spoiled it.

He asked me not to open any more!

Grampy said you're not meant to open runner beans if you're having them for Sunday lunch. You're supposed to leave them inside their green cases.

The **trouble with not opening runner beans** is you can't tell if there are any magic beans inside.

But Grampy still said, "Just pick them please, Daisy. Don't open them please, Daisy."

So I had to just pick them.

And not open them.

Not even one.

Which was totally Grampy's fault.

After about ten minutes we had twenty-one lovely long runner beans in our bowl. I really wanted to open them all, but Grampy said we must take them indoors and give them all to Nanny.

So we did.

Because he made me.

Chapter 17

I didn't want to give the runner beans to Nanny. Especially the ones I'd picked. I wanted to keep them for myself.

I didn't mind giving them to her once I'd opened them because then I could have checked to see if there were any magic beans inside.

But Grampy made me give Nanny ALL the beans.

Every one!

Nanny said we had done really well, and that as soon as she had whisked up her new Yorkshire pudding mix, she would top, tail and slice them ready for lunch.

Then Grampy and Mum started talking.

Then Nanny started whisking.

So I went back outside into the garden.

The **trouble with going into a garden after you've been picking beans** is it really makes you want to pick some more.

I mean, we had only picked about twenty in the first place, and there were still loads more dangling from the leaves.

There were long ones, short ones, thin ones, fat ones, big ones, little ones . . . Any one of them could have had a magic bean inside.

So I went back to the bamboo sticks and picked all the long ones I could reach.

I must have picked about fifty long ones before I had to start picking all the medium-sized ones.

Each time I pulled a runner bean from its stalk, I opened the green case and looked for a magic bean sparkling inside.

Trouble is, every bean I looked at just looked the same! Apart from the medium beans. They were just smaller.

So I had to pick all of Grampy's small beans too.

But they didn't have any sparkly beans in either. Some of them didn't even shine!

The really titchy ones didn't have any beans in at all!

Which only left the beans I couldn't reach.

So I went and got Grampy's wheelbarrow.

The **trouble with standing in Grampy's wheelbarrow** is it does make you able to reach higher, but if you lean over too far, it makes the wheelbarrow tip over.

Into the beans.

I was doing really well too. I only had one more bean to reach, but it was right under some leaves and really hard to get to, so I really had to stretch and streeeetch and streeeeeeeeeeeeeeeeeetch and . . .

. . . then the wheelbarrow fell over into the beans. With me in it.

The **trouble with falling into beans** is all the bamboo sticks fall over when you land on them and everything crashes to the ground.

At first I thought I was going to break something like my arm or my leg, but I didn't.

The only things I broke were Grampy's sticks. And some of his stalks.

Actually quite a lot of the stalks.

But I was all right. And the wheelbarrow was all right too.

When I had got up out of the beans, I looked across the garden towards the kitchen. The kitchen door was open, and I could see Mum and Grampy still talking. But no one came out.

So they obviously didn't mind.

So then I had a brilliant idea.

If there wasn't a magic bean in Grampy's garden, maybe there was a magic tomato! After all, if you can climb up to the clouds on a magic beanstalk, I'm sure you can do it on a magic tomato stalk!

So I picked all Grampy's tomatoes too. I didn't mean to. They just sort of kept coming off in my hand.

But they didn't sparkle either. They just stayed green and not that shiny.

And they made my fingers smell. So I needed to pick something else instead.

To get the smell off.

The **trouble with magic carrots** is the green bits at the top of them should sparkle.

But they don't. You have to pull the whole carrot out of the ground to see if the orange bit is sparkling underneath.

Even when you've pulled them out of the ground, you still can't tell straight away if they are magic or not, because the earth on them has to be rubbed off too.

I rubbed the earth off every one of Grampy's carrots, but I still couldn't find one that even slightly sparkled.

So I had to try his spring onions instead.

The **trouble with spring onions** is you think there is going to be much more of them under the ground when you pull, but there isn't.

I pulled up every single spring onion but there was hardly any onion growing underneath, and none of them looked magic at all.

There were only little white roots. Which isn't my fault.

So that only left the new potatoes and the lettuces.

The new potatoes were my favourite. When you pull them, all the earth comes up, and then it all sprinkles away to show you the potatoes underneath.

Sometimes you get loads! They're quite small and creamy-whitey coloured, and when you pull them, they come off their roots just like that!

If only they sparkled too!

But they didn't.

Not one single one of all Grampy's new potatoes was the slightest bit magic at all.

And as for his lettuces, well, they were just useless.

That's the **trouble with Grampy's vegetable garden**.

None of the vegetables are grown from magic seeds.

At least none of the vegetables I had looked at so far.

I was almost going to give up looking when I suddenly had

another good idea.

Well, it seemed like a good idea at the time.

I could look for magic vegetables in Grampy's greenhouse!

So I did.

Chapter 18

The **trouble with greenhouses** is they get really hot inside.

When I pulled back the glass door on Grampy's greenhouse, loads of hot heat came out all over me!

All the sunshine in the sky had made it hot enough inside to cook Yorkshire puddings in! And the smell was really funny too.

It smelled of mouldy flowerpots.

Once I'd let all the heat out, the smell started to go away.

Then I started to get used to it.

So I started looking for magic vegetables again.

There were lots of things growing in Grampy's greenhouse. They were all in trays with brown earth inside them, but I couldn't tell if they were vegetables or not. Because they were so small.

Which wasn't my fault.

Some had little things like cucumbers on them, plus big green leaves with yellow flowers.

Some trays had loads and loads
and loads of teensy green leaves on
teensy-weensy white stalks.

Those were the ones I pulled up first. You should have seen how easy they were to pull up!

I could do ten at once really easily. They just came right out in my hands, but none of them had sparkly roots below.

The little cucumbers didn't sparkle when I pulled them off either. Neither did the roots in the black trays, the red trays, or even the flowerpots when I tipped them upside down.

It was hopeless. There wasn't a magic vegetable anywhere. Nothing in Grampy's greenhouse sparkled at all. I had completely run out of ideas and vegetables.

Until I looked through the glass.

And saw the blackcurrants.

Chapter 19

The **trouble with blackcurrants** is if you squeeze them too hard, they pop.

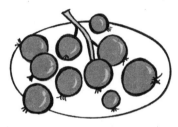

Especially very ripe blackcurrants.

At first I didn't know what a magic blackcurrant would be like, but then I worked it out.

A magic blackcurrant was bound to have special powers, so if you squashed it, it wouldn't pop.

So that's what I had to do. Squash all Grampy's blackcurrants.

The **trouble with squashing Grampy's blackcurrants** is if they pop too much, they pop all over you.

Like on your clothes.

If your clothes are your best clothes, then you don't really want blackcurrant juice on them at all.

Trouble is, I never noticed it was happening. I was too busy looking for the magic blackcurrant with

special powers to notice. Which isn't
my fault.

The person who noticed first of all was my mum.

"DAISY!!!!!" she said. Well, screamed more than said. **"WHAT ON EARTH DO YOU THINK YOU'RE DOING?!"**

So I said, "Looking for magic vegetables."

Then my grampy came out to see what Mum was shouting about.

You should have seen his face when he saw what I'd done.

"MY BEANS!" he said.

"MY TOMATOES!" he said.

"MY CARROTS!" he said.

"MY POTATOES!" he said.

"MY LETTUCES!" he said.

"MY SPRING ONIONS!" he said.

Then he went into the greenhouse.

"MY COURGETTES!" he said.

"MY MARROWS!" he said.

"MY SEEDLINGS!" he said.

Then he came out of the greenhouse.

"MY BLACKCURRANTS!" he said.

"YOUR BEST BLOUSE!" my mum said. Well, not said, but sort of shouted again.

Then I looked down at my best blouse and saw the blackcurrant juice that had popped all over it.

And then I went all sort of hot. And my fingers went all stiff. And my eyes went all watery.

Then my nanny came out to see what everyone was shouting about.

"MY WORD!" she said. "Daisy, whatever have you done?"

The **trouble with trying to explain about magic vegetables when your fingers are stiff and your eyes are watery** is, well . . . you can't think of what to say.

So I didn't say anything. At first.

My mum did. My mum didn't stop saying things for ages. She said I was a naughty naughty naughty girl and that if I didn't say sorry to Grampy straight away, she would never bring me to Nanny and Grampy's for Sunday lunch again.

Then my eyes went even waterier, and my tongue went all dry inside my mouth.

The first time I said sorry, no one heard me because my words were so quiet.

Then I said sorry *again.* A GIANT sorry. And then I started to cry.

The **trouble with crying** is sometimes it's really hard to stop.

Mum didn't care. She was far too cross to worry about my shoulders going up and down. She told me I had to help Grampy replant all the vegetables I had pulled up.

But Grampy said the sunshine would have dried the roots, so they wouldn't go back into the ground.

Then she said I would have to buy

Grampy some more seeds out of my own pocket money and help him plant every single one.

But Grampy said it was too late in the season to plant more seeds.

He asked me why I had pulled up all his vegetables, and I told him that I needed a magic bean, but a magic tomato would have worked, but there weren't any magic beans or tomatoes in his garden, however hard I looked or however hard I wished, so then all the other vegetables had made me get carried away, and so it really, really wasn't my fault!

Then he told me that if I was going to keep on crying, would I mind standing in the middle of the lawn because if I stood in the middle of the lawn, I'd make a lovely job of watering the grass.

Which made me laugh a bit. And smile a bit.

But I still felt ever so terrible. Because Grampy's vegetables looked ever so messy. And it was my fault really.

Nanny said she had to go back indoors because if she burned the Yorkshires again, that would be three disasters in one day.

Grampy said he'd plant some winter vegetables when he'd tidied up, and that maybe I'd like to help him when he'd bought the seeds.

I didn't really want to help him, because I'd gone right off vegetables for ever. But I dried my eyes and promised I would.

Mum gave me a tissue and told me to blow my nose. Then she banned me from playing giants for ever.

Including looking for magic beans.

Looking for magic vegetables.

Looking for magic fruit.

Or looking for magic anythings.

Then we went in for our lunch.

It was a very quiet Sunday lunch.
No one hardly said anything.

We just chewed.

And then we tidied away.

And then Mum and me went
home.

Chapter 20

When we got indoors, I went straight up to my room.

"PROMISE ME YOU WON'T PLAY GIANTS AGAIN, DAISY!" said Mum.

So I promised.

"I mean it, Daisy," said my mum. "If I hear so much as a Fee, a Fi, a Fo, or a Fum out of you, you are going to be in giant trouble!"

So I double promised.

Closed my bedroom door.

Sat on my bed.

Uncrossed my fingers.

Accidentally knocked my pillows onto the floor.

Turned them into clouds.

Picked up my hundred-metre blue biro.

And wrote a secret letter to Jack Beechwhistle!

A secret letter to:
Jack Beechwhistle
Castle in the Sky
Above the clouds

Dear Jack,
No one must know I'm writing this letter, because my mum will go mad if she finds out.

I'm writing to you to tell you some bad news.

My mum says I'm banned from being a giant any more, which means so is Wendy the Whopping. Because being giants in the first place was my idea, so she's not allowed to play it without me.

I'm a bit sad, because being giants was really good fun.

Especially the bit when I picked

you up out of the sweetshop and threw you into the dunjon of our castle in the sky.

I reckon my mum will let me be a giant again one day, when she has carmed down a bit. But it may be quite a long time.

Giant dunjon keys are very massiv, which means they can only be picked up by giants. So I won't be able to let you out again until I'm a giant again.

Which is even more bad news. Because you'll have to stay in the dunjon for about a hundred years now.

Sorry.

But actually, it serves you right for being horrible to Daniel.

Love Hannah the Highest(Daisy x)

P.S. THERE ARE EGGS IN THE FRIDGE.

DAISY'S TROUBLE INDEX

The trouble with . . .

More than a million

DAISY

books sold!

Kes Gray (The author of Oi FROG!)

DAISY

and the trouble with
BURGLARS